Don't Stay Too Long
By The River

by

Cee McAdams

WingSpan Press

Published in the United States and the United Kingdom
by WingSpan Press, Livermore, CA

The WingSpan name, logo and colophon are the trademarks
of WingSpan Publishing.

ISBN 978-1-63683-044-5 (pbk.)
ISBN 978-1-63683-497-9 (hardcover)
ISBN 978-1-63683-965-3 (ebk.)

Printed in the United States of America

www.wingspanpress.com

Books by Cee McAdams:

Mile High Tales (out of print)

Low Hanging Branches

Cloud Cover

Qtr Moon Mysteries

Journey

In The Garden Of Moonlight

Don't Look Back

"You may feel like leaving home is the anchor in your storm but leaving may well save you from drowning."

—Home Stratosphere

"I spoke to the river and the river spoke back to me...It said man you look so lonely...You look full of misery..."

—Percy Mayfield

Chapter 1

Not much planning went into a trip into the village for supplies circa 1881...you just hitched up the wagon and off you went. My Mom always had her list ready and father usually handled the team...on this day, father was busy with other matters and it was just Mom and me. I liked to chat with the animals along the way but today none of them wanted to make conversation so I had nothing to do except handle my driving and anticipate getting a surprise, usually hard candy or sometimes apples.

That day began no differently. We parked the wagon underneath the tree and went inside to buy the supplies. When we were done, Mom handed me a small bag of hard candy as my reward. I popped a piece into my mouth and began to make the trips back and forth to the wagon to load the supplies.

On our way back to the wagon with the last of the supplies, three men appeared and began to heckle my mother.

My Mom was a beautiful woman, about 4 feet 10 inches tall, maybe a hundred ten pounds, hair like woven silk which she always wore in a braid, either wound around her head or hanging down to her waist. She had a way of walking that made her appear to glide gracefully. She sometimes wore a serious expression when she was anticipating unpleasantness but she had an infectious smile that complimented her effervescent personality. To me, she was Mom who always seemed to smell like the jasmine that grew near our house...to these men, she was an object of ridicule, or a thing to toy with, like a large cat playing with a half dead mouse.

The men began to make comments about my mom like 'she sure is purrty' and 'what is that smell'? My father would have told me to ignore them but he was not there so I told them to back off and go about their business; they only ignored me and continued to make lewd comments about my Mom. Finally, one of the men, the one wearing dirty farmers' coveralls, with teeth that looked like jagged rock, an ear that looked like a piece of banana peel that had been left out in the sun and a gopher had chewed on it, and skin that looked like a rough muddy road - in fact, he was as ugly as a mud fence, referred to my mom as a squaw. I walked right up to him and asked him politely to apologize, but this only brought about raucous laughter from him and his 2 friends as if that was the world's best joke. I tried to remain calm as I listened to the drumming of my heart, but I could feel my pulse pounding and my anger rising.

My father always carried a hunting knife and I wished that he had been there at that moment but he was not around so I had to rely on my own wits and just my 2 fists, hoping that these men would just be done with their fun and move on...apparently, they had other things in mind.

They began to circle me like vultures over a carcass, obviously not concerned about their advantage, 3 grown men against one gangly teenage boy and one small woman. I picked up a rock and balled my fist around it. The other 2 men said something to each other and then turned and went into the store. The one with the chewed-on ear continued to shout obscenities and point at us as he came closer.

Behind him was a large barrel which I thought contained apples but out of the corner of my eye, I saw a wisp of smoke coming from the top. He moved in closer until he was maybe 8 feet from me when he called my mom 'a filthy squaw.' My anger boiled over and I threw the rock at him but missed as he ducked...he charged at me but I was quicker...I sidestepped him and then grabbed him by the neck, locking him in the bend of my elbow and began to squeeze...he struggled as I watched him turn a mottled shade of green. He tried to claw at my arms but I only tightened my grip...as we struggled, we moved backwards closer to the barrel...I clamped down harder...only when he stopped struggling that I loosen my grip and realized that he didn't seem to be breathing. I dragged him over to the barrel and took a quick peek inside and was surprised to learn that it did not contain apples...I lifted him off his feet and dumped him inside of it where something smelly was still smoldering...just where he belonged.

My mom had a hold of my arm and was yelling something unintelligible as she pulled me back to the wagon and all but shoved me in just as the other two were coming out of the store with ax handles...suddenly we were racing away from the trading post and my Mom was muttering something to herself, probably saying her prayers.

We raced back to our home nearly turning the wagon over as the excited and frightened horses picked up speed. I could hardly slow them down as we dashed into the yard. My father, who was out by the toolshed, turned at the sound of the commotion and ran over to help stop the horses. My Mom was as pale as a ghost as my father lifted her from the wagon and helped her into the house. I was busy trying to get the supplies unloaded when he came out to ask what had happened.

My throat had constricted and I felt as if there was a gallon of molten lava in the pit of my stomach that was threatening to spew...I held up a sack, ran into the house and collapsed on the first chair I saw. After I could catch my breath, I told my father the story about the incident at the trading post. My Mom was nodding as I replayed what had happened. When I was finished, they both looked at me with sadness in their eyes and then at each other... they had decided almost at the same moment, that I was going to have to leave home as quickly as possible because the people from the village would be coming for me...it all settled in on me like a heavy fog...I realized, that even at 16, my life as I knew it, was over.

Chapter 2

About an hour before nightfall, with stars winking in the barely night sky in September, I set out to find another fugitive from a neighboring village who would become my traveling companion. No one explained to me why another person, another young man, had landed in such unfortunate circumstances but I suppose I was relieved to know that I would not be traveling alone.

Leaving was hard and I wanted to spend as much time with my parents as possible because I knew I may never see them again, so I dawdled as long as I could. My Mom hugged me and cried a lot but said only a few words. My dad was more afraid for my safety than he let on so he walked with me a little way, offering me a few words of wisdom and encouragement, and then abruptly turned and ran back...I think it was because he didn't want me to see the tears on his face...I had to fight the powerful urge not to run back with him.

Before leaving, my parents and the neighbors had combined what food, water and a few pieces of silver, the little they could afford, and packed it in a flour sack, along with at least one change of clothing and the only other pair of shoes I owned. Since I had grown up around there, I knew the area and knew there was ample water, berries, nuts in the forest and trout in the rivers and small streams...my father gave me his hunting knife but I was not going to harm the animals unless or until it became necessary, as an act of absolute desperation.

I met up with fugitive number 2 about a half mile from my house. He was as scared and disheveled as I was, just two lost souls on our way to no place we knew. Neither of us carried a lantern so the only available light was from the moon and the millions of winking stars. By the time we reached the river, it was nearly dark but we could see by the moonlight as it danced in the water.

I had initially decided that it would be safer to travel by the light of the moon but now that there were two of us, we put our ideas together to try to plot our course. Not being men of sophistication or having much imagination, we chatted about which way to go but soon ran out of steam and figured that we would just follow the trail. What to call ourselves became the next puzzle to solve... we selected names of animals and birds and all manner things but none of them seemed to fit...we settled on Blue and Green and didn't give it any further thought...I was going to be called Green and my traveling companion was going to be called Blue...after all, if we get the opportunity to contact our parents, they will know our names.

We stood there for a while and stared into the water...I spoke about my troubles and how I hated leaving my home...Blue was afraid to talk about how he had ended up on this goodbye road alongside me...he kept looking around, peering into the darkness, speaking in near whispers, always on the verge of tears, seemingly afraid he would be discovered and killed on the spot. I didn't press him on it...I had my own burden to bear, the turbulence in my heart and that great feeling of despair was nearly paralyzing. I could tell that he was dealing with great sadness and I could only hope that he would not turn back and leave me to go alone.

After a few moments to allow the shakes to subside, I sat by the river and allowed my thoughts to run free, each one tumbling over the other. I wanted to build a fire but knew that would be a foolish thing to do so I wrapped myself in the warmth of the stars and the moonlight...I was reminded of my Mom's warning so I dared not fall asleep.

The next morning, the sun came racing over the horizon and if to catch us unaware. I was momentarily mesmerized by the beauty of our surroundings and by the audacity of the sun. We had agreed to travel mostly by night but now it seemed so long ago since we started out, and having spent one night alone in the forest, we were willing to reconsider... we were both restless, impossible to get comfortable...

there were things in the woods that could see us but that we could not see at night, not just the hunters we believed to be on our trail...we were going to have to come up with a different plan.

We had not gone far when I heard noises... we stood stock-still and held onto each other like frightened children...we had to find cover but there was no place to hide except behind a tree or a cluster of bushes. Blue had a look of sheer terror which had frozen on his face...I had to practically drag him along, pleading with him not to make any noise.

We hid as best we could behind some bushes draped in vines with broken logs strewn around. Blue was whimpering so I held him close and tried to smother the sound so he would not be heard...I was too afraid to risk standing to take a look so we waited. Waiting was painful. I could hear voices but they were muted and I could not hear what they were saying....it could not have taken more than a few minutes for the voices to fade but it felt like hours. Finally, I stood to take a look once I could no longer hear the voices...as it turned out, these were just a couple of people, a man and boy, perhaps his kid, in a canoe looking for a good place to fish... they never saw me but I saw the poles sticking out of the canoe.

I breathed a sigh of relief as we eased out of our pitiful excuse for a hiding place but knew we were going to have to quicken our pace and get out of this part of the woods before we were discovered by the wrong someone... people were no doubt already looking for me...it would not take long for word to get around that we were probably together and we would both be doomed... there was no place to go and no one to ask for help in these woods...we were on our own and the situation felt hopeless.

We kept to the woods and made good time, stopping by a stream here or a pond there just to catch our breath, have a snack and get a drink. By nightfall, we were miles away from home and feeling a bit safer, but only a bit. Any minute now we were expecting to hear the sound of bloodhounds following our trail but thankfully so far, we had missed that pleasure. Blue had relaxed a little but still kept his thoughts mostly to himself.

Blue was an artist and would stop and draw pictures whenever we were at a sandy spot in the road...he drew pictures mostly of his family but sometimes just whatever appeared in his mind's eye. He would sometimes decorate them with leaves for eyebrows and use a bit of grass for hair....the effect was quite startling. I think this helped to ease his feelings of homesickness and outrage at the situation. I understood but there was no time for brooding about it...I admired the pictures and then it was time to move on...we knew night would be upon us again soon and we had to find a way to stay alive.

We waded deeper into the woods by the light of the sun by day and the moon and the stars by early night. The woods were full of dangerous things like bears and rattlers so we tried to stay away from boggy areas and stick to what amounted to a trail of sorts, even climbed a tree when there was one suitable as a place to sit. The weather was cooperating with us so far and we were grateful for that...there was nowhere to hide from a storm out in those woods but now and then I would catch the slightest whisp of a breeze and try to hold it in our lungs forever...it made me a bit giddy but the moment always passed quickly.

By the following evening, we were certain that we were far enough away to venture out of the woods just long enough to find a settlement and buy some food...our meager provisions were only meant to last a day or two...considering that we were almost on the brink of panic, we had absentmindedly eaten more of our provisions than we should have.

We were trudging along, Blue humming to himself...I was keeping my eyes on the trail but dreaming of a nice cool swim when suddenly I was yanked from my wool gathering by a slow moving turtle...it had a head like a gnarled root with eyes, and it was red underneath...Blue rushed over to have a look and informed me that they were all around and nothing to be afraid of...the little guy was probably just on his way home or simply trying to find water. I'm sure he felt right at home...it was me who was lost...I had not gotten out and away from home enough to be familiar with the wildlife...this little turtle was new to me.

We had not gone more than a half mile from where we left the turtle when I was assaulted by the smell of smoke. I remembered that my parents had a smoke house where they smoked hams and other meat and hung it up on hooks...I wondered just how close we were to a settlement and if anyone had some smoked ham...not that it mattered, we could not afford to buy any... still a guy can dream and have his mouth water from the memory...the lure of food was a powerful magnet and almost overwhelming... we had to decide if we should risk a visit and which one of us should go in...I could not leave Blue alone but was afraid to go without him. Finally we decided to wait until just before the store closed and then go in together...we would check our measly coin and buy only the barest of necessities. Even though we didn't know it yet, we were about to get more than just a little food...we were about to walk right into a hornet's nest.

We waited and watched as people left the store, 2 men and what appeared to be a young girl around the age of 10. They did not seem to be in a great hurry as they disappeared around the side of the building. We decided that this was as good a time as any. We tried not to hurry but Blue was so nervous that he kept stumbling, colliding with me and nearly knocking me off my feet. We eased into the store, the hinges making a slight screaming sound as we opened the door, long overdue for a bit of oil on the hinges. We carefully chose two items each, a can of beans and an apple and hurried to the counter to pay so we could disappear as quickly as possible, but as we waited for the owner to take our money, we realized that it was taking a very long time...perhaps he went into the back for something and was taking a while for him to come to the front.

I was sweating and Blue was fidgeting, bouncing from one foot to the other...waiting was excruciating...I could all but hear my nerves jangling and tingling. When I could stand the waiting no longer, I looked around and finally peered over the counter and saw someone lying on the floor... without realizing that my feet were moving, I rushed out of the door, still clutching the two items I had picked up...Blue was right on my heels.

Someone had obviously visited this store earlier and had killed or badly wounded the owner...I did not take the time to examine his wounds...he was not moving and to me that meant dead. It was possibly and most likely the people we saw leaving just before we went in. It conjured up the image I had tried and failed to put out of my mind of the old guy back at the village, who looked like a weasel and had skin like dry boot leather, lying crumpled in that barrel...dead or not, it made no difference in the horror or the urgency of my situation...I am again with another victim who will surely be laid in my lap, either just me or both Blue and me...

we had no choice but to run fast and get as far away from there as we could before this one was discovered.

We ran back to where we had left our packs and dumped the items inside... then we tossed them over our shoulders and took off like lightning. The sun was dropping, just a smear of orange sherbet still remained so we knew we couldn't go far before we would have to find some place to camp for the night. I was in unfamiliar territory now, no real feel for this area of the forest. I heard dogs yapping but only thought they were dogs at someone's home and not those that would have been on our trail...still I had to be alert and to try to look after Blue...I was beginning to feel like the big brother.

We came out of the woods into a small clearing and I saw what could have been the most amazing building I had ever seen. It looked sad and forlorn as though it had been many years since it had seen a visitor or had a coat of paint...it was leaning slightly and the only door was hanging by one hinge...it was most likely an abandoned barn but it was beautiful. The roof remained in place and we could hardly wait to get in there...this was going to be home for as long as we could afford to stay or at least we hoped.

I approached cautiously...the door swung open with a screech, protesting loudly at being bothered after so long a time...a fat ray of sunlight revealed dust motes and spider's webs three yards wide. I picked up a stick to use to clear out the spider's webs but it fell apart in my hand...I looked around for another one but before I could pick it up, a familiar sound alerted me to movement in the corner...I pointed in that direction so that Blue could see him too...we had disturbed a rattler dining on a large rat and he was letting us know that he had no intention of sharing.

I had a hunting knife but I thought it best to just let him finish his dinner and then chase him away...we were going to be moving in and did not want his company...if he objected, then we would have to make a choice – leave or fight...luckily for us, he chose to leave...he didn't like our attitudes and didn't want to share his dinner so he slithered out of a hole in the wall, maybe the same one he had crawled through earlier.

This place had a window on each side which amazingly had not been broken out...they were narrow, with years of dirt and grime... one was slightly raised a small crack but otherwise solid...it also had a window in the upper space. I cautiously climbed up the old creaking ladder to investigate and found several partial bales of hay but there was nothing else of immense interest except that if we chose to sleep up here, we could see someone coming for about half a mile. I climbed back down and gave that some thought. Next I found an old rake and cleared out some of the old dried trash and junk so I that I could see the floor...then Blue went through the stuff in the back on the shelves and found several treasures: an old machete, about 9 feet of rope, a large thick tarp, a canteen, fishing gear, an old pail, matches in a metal tin, three pair of cover-alls that must have belonged to someone twice our size, jars of preserved fruit, mostly peaches, one old boot and a lantern almost full of oil...he even found change in one of the pockets of the coveralls...he dumped it all in a pile on the floor so we could have a better look...we could hardly contain our joy and great fortune.

After I swept the floor [with the rake] the best I could, we spread out the tarp, and rolled up two pair of the coveralls for make-shift pillows...then we took a look at our palace. There were too many cracks to try to cover them all so we put partial bales of hay over the larger ones and used whatever sticks and rocks we could find, even the old boot, to cover most of the others. We de-cided this would have to do. The windows would let enough light come through so we would use the lantern only as a necessity. I dragged the door closed on its one remain-ing hinge which groaned as if it were in great pain, used the rope to tie it so it would remain closed, propped the rake against it and settled in...home sweet home!

We ate canned fruit until our eyes bulged... we knew we would have to find the river the next day, maybe catch a trout or two and refill our canteens...we were almost out of water.

I was totally stuffed so after I finished eating, I passed out from sheer exhaustion. It had not been my intention to fall asleep on the lower floor.

The last I remember was Blue talking about staying here for a week or so or until we ran completely out of provisions or until the moon turned to dust. Then I was transported into a dream of nightmarish proportions.

I was running but going nowhere, seemingly bogged down in knee-deep mud except I could see no mud...I was being chased by a horde of very large, very tall birds that could have been turkeys except they had 2 heads with sunken yellow eyes and were about 6 feet tall. They had talons that were extremely long and sharp and gleamed in the sun. Two of them were leading dogs on leashes and the dogs were snarling and drooling and pulling at their leashes as the birds shrieked. I could see that they were gaining on me so I tried again to pull my feet free so that I could move, run. There were trees ahead...if I could only make it to the trees, I might have a chance to survive... turkeys can't fly and I didn't think those dogs would be able to climb a tree...I didn't know whether or not turkeys could climb trees...I guess I was about to find out.

It was scorching hot...I could feel the heat settle around my mouth and nose as if I had stepped inside of a blazing fire...I couldn't scream or even call out because my throat was clogged with thick acrid smoke...I was having trouble breathing and could feel my heart thundering like a herd of wilder beast...I could almost feel the skin on my face melting...suddenly the fire seemed to die down a bit and there was a slight breeze which brought with it the most putrid smell imaginable... .propelled by the image of becoming a dead thing, left to rot and be a part of this smell, picked apart by the strange bird-things, I yanked my feet free and began running as fast as I could. I reached the trees, or rather a large tree but it was already occupied with many bodies, from the lowest limb to the very top...there was no room for me.

At this realization I was convinced that I had soiled myself but there was no time to stop to check...I ran, more out of terror than from the thought of embarrassment, since I saw only the strange bird-things and was sure they would not have an opinion...I ran blindly and stumbled into a small creek where I fell face-first. The water was cool, almost cold, and the splashing woke me with a start, gasping for breath.

I sat up and took stock of my surroundings. I was soaking wet. I was still in the little shack and Blue was asleep a few feet away. It must have been close to sunrise because light was grudgingly trying to stream through the windows. I climbed up to have a look, to see if any remnants of my nightmare were lurking outside...I didn't see anything except what appeared to be a small stream or a pond directly in back of the shack a few yards away and to the left...I hurried down and out the door to investigate; it was not an illusion...it was an oasis! I can't imagine how I missed it when we arrived the evening before...perhaps because it was nearly dark and I don't have owl vision.

I went back inside to get the canteens, to see if I could first get fresh water, then take a short dip. I felt a little guilty about waking Blue but could not contain my great joy...he jumped up and gave me that glassy-eyed stare as if I were a monster out of his own nightmare...he eventually staggered out of the door, still half asleep, but followed me to the edge of the stream... glaring at it wild-eyed and in disbelief, he started to take off his shoes and shirt but I told him my idea of filling our canteens first.

Up until now, Blue had been a guy of few words but suddenly he was giggling and babbling like a kid who had just gotten a brand-new toy. After we filled all of the canteens, we splashed around in the water for an hour or so...I could feel all of the fear and tension melting away as I swam back and forth...with much hesitation, we finally climbed out and put on clean clothes...I had lost track of just how many days we had been in those same clothes...I think, more than Blue, I really needed a swim. I decided not to tell him about my nightmare. I could not tell how far away from home we were or how much farther we would have to travel so I figured later would be a better time...Blue was already on edge, with good reason, as well as being a bit squeamish and I still had tendrils of fear that curled around my heart every now and then... staying calm and vigilant was key to staying alive. I allowed him to enjoy this moment...we may not get another one.

We spent the better part of the morning wandering around the area, watching morning slowly creep into the afternoon but not straying too far from the shack, trying to decide if we should try to catch some fish...since we had already found the stream, there was not much left to discover except more woods. I was no longer terrified of being stalked by friends of the raving maniac back in the other village but I also knew we were still fugitives and as such, still worried about building a fire, knowing it would attract attention, perhaps the wrong kind, so cooking fish over an open fire didn't seem to be a smart idea...going into another settlement was too risky so we decided that we would have to make out on what we had for another day or two...we had shelter, canned peaches and a source of water...this should have given me a profound sense of comfort but it filled me instead with a sense of dread that we would get too comfortable, let our guard down and be discovered or killed in our sleep...I involuntarily shivered at the thought of searing pain or being drowned in thick black water filled with green slime and choking on live baby water moccasins.

I can hardly close my eyes without having thoughts that come barreling through my head of why I'm in this place...it was all such bad timing and worse luck, but there is no way to stop the memories from hammering my every waking moment and some of the time when I'm not awake. This was hardly my idea of adventure, having to leave my home...I miss my home and my family and most of all, I miss my Mom's cooking. I left her with sorry and fear in her heart with no way to ease her worry and anxiety...I thought of where I would go and who would listen to my story, that is, if I ever found the courage to even tell it...would I get out of this forest alive and find people who have regular lives that will share them with me? I'm having these thoughts as we are lying on the floor of our palace, listening to the thunder and the crack of the lightening, waiting for the storm to roll in, grateful that we are not still out in the woods.

I have tried many times to engage Blue in conversation as a way to pass the time and I try again to get him to feel a bit closer to me, but he is a keeper of secrets, not a word about why he is on this perilous hike into nowhere alongside me...he only mentioned that he had to leave his dog, a small black lab that he named Cotton, and wondered if he would ever see him again...then silence would take over again as I watched a tremor pass through him. His storm was raging inside of him.

There were lightning flashes farther away at first and then a moment later, much closer and accompanied by a rumble and then a peal of thunder nearly on top of us. Dust and bits and pieces of hay drifted down as the storm intensified. Once again that finger of dread poked me in the pit of my soul...I feared that someone would see this place and think of it as a refuge from the storm... we would surely be discovered...I told myself that all I would have to do is explain that we were simply waiting out the storm and then we would move on, but secretly I was praying that everyone else was safely tucked into his own home and we would be left alone and be able to stay here a little while longer.

The storm is fully upon us now, drumming on the metal roof of our palace... I can hear the wind howling in the trees...I am grateful that we have shelter and also grateful that Blue is with me even though he is not much of a conversationalist. Water is falling through a small crack in the roof but it was over on the side of the room away from where we were lying on our tarp. Blue got up and put the pail underneath the leak so that we could catch the water and save it for use a little later.

Chapter 3

Something nudged me awake...not a sound or a presence but an unknown sensation... it was not Blue...he was still sleeping peacefully. I stood up, stretched and tried to find the source of this strange and ominous feeling...it hung on for nearly five minutes and then seemed to vanish like a soft breeze. I realized that it was no longer raining – all I heard was the sound of absolute silence. I opened the door gently and saw a startlingly beautiful day. The rain had left the air fresh and clean and I tried to take in as much as I could, wishing that it would give me hope, courage and new resolve...Mom once told me that hope was tenuous and deceptive...Mom may have been right but right now, hope is all that I've got to hang on to.

I didn't want to leave the place we had

come to think of as our palace but I know that it was time for us to move on. I knew it will be hard to convince Blue that this was not home, that it had only been temporary shelter from the storm... now that the storm had passed , we needed to find whatever is between here and wherever we may finally settle. I think of my family and hope that I can find a way to contact them, especially my Mom to let her know that I'm OK...not well fed but alive and as well as could be expected.

We began to gather up our meager belong-ings and made sure we had the matches... we used the water we collected in the pail to clean ourselves as best we could...neither of us complained that we were not daisy-fresh. We finished the last of the peaches for breakfast so that we could travel a little ways before hunger zapped our strength. We refilled all of our canteens including the one that had been left behind, tempted to take one last swim. Instead, I just closed the door and then we set off again, feeling a bit sad for a different reason...we had a few more belongings than when we started but we had them folded into a bundle so that we could sling them over our shoulder. Along the way, we may find great need for the tarp and the machete...we brought along the lantern as well, just in case.

We walked at a much slower pace than before, for what felt like hours and saw a totally unobstructed view of blue sky and then suddenly we were in woods so dense that we could not see ten feet in front of us. I am not sure but I think that we may have crossed the Alabama state line and that we were in Mississippi...the mosquitos were as big as vampire bats and just as persistent about having us provide a snack for them... there must be water, a swamp perhaps, to provide them with a source of constant nourishment. I was unfamiliar with that part of the world...I didn't recognize the trees or the fruit they were bearing. I didn't see any berries or pecan trees or anything edible. I could not follow the river because I didn't know where the river would lead, even if I found the river...I knew we would cross it sooner or later...but then it was a mystery. I had to stay out of the tree cover as much as possible so that I could get my bearings, which way was North, which way was West and which way would lead me to freedom and peace of mind...food was always on my mind and panic was never far away.

I walked along the edge of the woods and suddenly there was a sound... not just a sound, a bell, a church bell. I looked around but saw no church...it must have been farther away and beyond the woods where we were standing. I wondered if it was Sunday... if so, then I had been away from home for 7 days I think, maybe 8 or more...it could have been a year...I had lost all sense of days and hours, only the time spent plodding along, lost in my own thoughts. I had all but given up on trying to get Blue to unburden his soul, thinking that it would make the nightmare easier to endure... perhaps his pain was still too raw and that his emotional devastation was much deeper than I could possibly know and that it would take a lot longer to heal, or perhaps he knew or sensed that I was not the person with whom to share his pain since I was also teetering on the edge of the abyss.

For reasons I didn't fully understand, Blue decided to take the lead...this was not un-pleasant, just surprising, so I moved along in my own heavy-footed way at my own pace. I must have been wool-gathering again be-cause suddenly I bumped into Blue who had stopped and stood as still as a statue. He was looking a bit bewildered and the sound that came from him was like the voice of doom. He was pointing so I stepped around him and took a look. There, about twenty feet in front of us, was a cemetery, not very well kept but not entirely overgrown with weeds and vines...some of the monuments looked as if they were struggling to remain upright...others had long-since forgotten flowers that had died and dried up from the sun... directly across the way and down the hill, was a church and the obvious source of the bell.

I could see that it was a small church and there were people filing inside, dressed in what my Mom would consider Sunday clothes. It was a small settlement with other buildings nearby including a small store with the sign that advertised General Merchandise, no doubt a combination of feed, hardware and grocery like the one in the village near my former home. Farther down was what appeared to be a stable or a corral or a place to keep the animals, and other buildings I could not see or identify from that distance. A million thoughts crossed my mind but I could not get them to line up in any kind of logical fashion. I glanced at Blue but he was standing as still as if he were being held in place...after a long moment, he just turned and ran back the way we had come, sat down on a fallen log, buried his face in his hands and made a sound somewhere between a sigh and a moan, something unexplainable.

The sun had successfully climbed over the trees and sunlight was slanting through the limbs that were just thinking about shedding their leaves. Blue was sitting on a log doing a kind of whimpering...I sat beside him and tried to console him, although I had no real idea why he was in such distress... we were in an unknown area and certainly couldn't know any of the people but somehow, I didn't think that was the reason for his strange behavior...all I could see was the cemetery so perhaps the sight of the cemetery both saddened and frightened him. I asked what was wrong and he stopped whimpering long enough to tell me a story that was right out of his worst nightmare... he said he never thought he would actually see a cemetery or come face to face with any part of that story.

My first thought was that it was one of those stories elders tell kids to entertain them at bedtime or to get them to huddle together out of fear and fall asleep, but according to Blue, this was not that kind of story...it was about an old soldier who had been killed in battle but during his final moments, he expressed that he had longed to go home to see his family again. According to the story, each night he would rise and wander about, peering through windows, trying to see if his loved ones were inside, without much success. Sometimes the old soldier would actually go inside homes to examine the faces of those who were sleeping there but when he did not find his loved ones, he would simply leave the way he had entered. By this time, he was hardly more than bones, and his uniform was just rags torn in strips. Blue claimed that one night he saw this old soldier. His eyes were hollow as he looked through the window into Blue's room. His fingers were nothing more than bones that looked like burnt twigs as he pointed them at Blue. There were no teeth but the jaws opened to reveal the maw of the head of a skeleton. Blue said he was too terrified to scream so he hid underneath his blankets, shaking with fear, too afraid to leave his room and run to his parents...he stayed hidden until the next morning when the sun was up and all he could see was blue sky.

The next morning, once he could finally get his teeth to stop chattering and his tongue to work, he tried to tell his dad about what he had seen the night before. After a long

moment, his dad just shook his head, somewhat in disbelief but did confirm that there
had been such a story about a wandering
soldier whose name had been Ben or Bart
or Benny something - he couldn't remember if he had ever heard a last name, especially since he believed the story to be
nothing more than superstitious nonsense
- who had been killed during the civil war...
it was only the stuff of legend, his dad had
told him, like fishing tales where the fish
just keep getting bigger and bigger. No
one had actually seen the supposed wandering soldier, but every now and then, this
story would surface and the legend would
continue to grow. Blue's dad tried to assure
him that he had probably seen nothing
more than tree branches scraping against
the window and the eerie sound of the wind
blowing plus the over-active imagination of
a teenage boy...once his imagination kicked
in, his eyes started playing tricks on him,
nothing more.

Blue had listened to his dad's explanation
but said he had no doubt that he had looked

into those hollow eyes and had seen exactly what he feared he had seen. He then, wiped his face, raised his arm and pointed a shaky finger toward the cemetery and said that the name on one of those monuments was Benny something, just as in the story...I decided to take a look for myself.

The ground around the monument was a bit spongy but not entirely covered with moss and grass...I tried to step lightly so as not to disturb any part of the soil around it but feeling as if this were a bizarre kind of investigation. I leaned over to get as close as I could, trying desperately not to tip over...the headstone was slightly leaning and looked as if it had been moved aside and not put back in the exact place as before...it had been damaged from years of rain, baking in the sun and other kinds of weather...there was a thin layer of something that looked like soot on top of it and there was a name etched on it, Bennington "Benny" Lowdon. It sent an icy shiver down my spine.

I went back and sat beside Blue again...I had no explanation or words of comfort to offer him so I just sat there with my arm around his shoulder. After a short while, he stopped shaking, stood up and looked around and if to find a way around this place so that he would not have to look at that monument again. Thankfully, the moment of terror and despair had mostly passed and his pit of depression had been a shallow one... it was time to move on and let this poor old soldier rest in peace if he could...Blue just wanted to go home...unfortunately, that was not one of our options.

The cemetery was on a small hill but the settlement was close, about a quarter of a mile. At this time of the day, it was mostly quiet, only the slight sound of singing coming from the church. I thought about going into the settlement to ask for work but Blue would have to agree to go as well and he was still afraid. Neither one of us had ever been in a real town but this one did not seem like a busy bustling village to me. I told him that I would wait until the people came out of the church and then see if the store was open and what I could buy with my few coins or ask the storekeeper for work. Between us, we had very little money and was almost completely out of food. I wasn't exactly trembling with anticipation... in fact, I was almost as frightened as he was but I knew that sooner rather than later, our stomachs would remind us that they were empty...a decision had to be made...I would have to swallow my fear in order to abate my hunger and try to convince Blue that he should consider doing the same.

I made my way down the hill to the village on rubbery knees, stepping around large rocks and picking my way through scrub bushes. My pulse was hammering a staccato in my ears and made my breath catch and my chest hurt...it felt as if I had swallowed a porcupine and the quills were rattling in protest and I struggled just to stay on my feet. Blue was tugging on my arm and pleading with me to turn around and go back...I opened my mouth to speak but no words came out...I could only shake my head sadly and continue down the hill...Blue followed along but he was certainly not wearing a happy face.

Church services were just ending and some-one I assumed was the general store owner was headed toward his store...I was still in the street but near the store when he walked up, unlocked the door and stepped inside. I tried to ignore the knot of fear that burned like an inferno in the pit of my stomach so I took a deep stuttering breath and followed him a step or two. He turned and looked at Blue and me with a kind of twisted sneer on his face but did not say a word. After a long painful moment, he asked us to come in.

The story keeper was not wearing a friendly expression when he asked me what he could do for me but I thought I caught the slight-est hint of a grin trying to make its way to the corner of his mouth, as if he had thought of a wicked joke but wasn't ready to spring it on me just yet. I said that we were just passing through town and wanted to know if he had any work that we could do...[I suppose I should have said for room and board but those were not words that were familiar to me at the time.] Blue said nothing, just stood frozen in his tracks. He looked us both up and down and finally led us to the back of his store. He said that he had needed help around the store but the right time or person had not come along. He pointed to a lot of sacks and crates and said that he would pay us to move them from here to there and later some of it would have to be put inside the store on shelves. He told us to put our bags over in the corner and that we could start work right away.

I worked until my belly began to rumble, so loudly that the storekeeper could have heard it...he came and told us that we could go over to a place down the street and get a meal for 15 cents, and with another 5 cents, we could get a slice of apple pie. He gave us two bits each and told us that it would be our pay for the day but that he expected us to come back and do more work until we had moved all of the sacks to their rightful place.

Off we went, tired but feeling as if we were walking on clouds, having money in our pockets and the idea of going into a place to eat all by ourselves. We sat down slowly and wondered if at any minute someone would order us to leave...no one did but someone came and asked us what we would like...there was a sign for beef stew that made my mouth water with anticipation so I ordered that for each of us plus 2 slices of apple pie. All of it was delicious and gone way too quickly. I thought we were most likely in heaven but I didn't see any angels.

I went back to the store with a full stomach, but the knot of apprehension had relaxed only slightly. The storekeeper, Mr. DeSayeo, told us that we could get back to work but that there was no hurry. In fact, he invited us to pull up a crate and have a seat. I held my breath and waited for him to ask why two young men were out wandering around by ourselves but instead he just smiled, asked our names and began talking to us, mostly about the weather and the crops and stuff in general but eventually he got around to talking about himself, about how long he had been in that part of the country and how he had come to settle in the village. He said that he had been with an uncle early on but that his uncle had been killed during the war. When he realized that he had no one, he just wandered around and found work when possible, doing whatever he could do to feed himself. Eventually he taught himself to write, read and count money.

He told us that one day he stopped to help an old man who appeared to have been ill and was having trouble with his team of horses...Mr. DeSayeo said that he had helped him to his store which was hardly more than a barn at that time. He helped the old man get inside and into bed. He ran errands for him and heated up cans of food he could find plus whatever the neighbors brought for him to eat. He spent his days looking after the old man until he passed away. Feeling lost and with no place else to go, he decided to just stay and keep the store going, at least for a while.

The old man had told him that he had no family and that the wagon, team and store would be his, but since he had no sort of ownership papers, he was always afraid that one day someone from the old man's family would turn up and demand what was his or hers. After so many years went by, Mr. De-Sayeo told us that he had ownership of the store and that he was an accepted member of the community. When we showed up, however, he was a little worried at first, thinking maybe we would be those long-lost family members about to make an unreasonable demand for his store. Once he realized that was not our purpose, he told us that he was happy to help us as someone had once helped him...good deeds beget good deeds, he told us.

Mr. DeSayeo talked for almost 30 minutes and finally told us that we could sleep in his barn for the night if we did not have the price of a room at the boarding house down the street. I told him that we did not and thanked him for his generous offer...he assured us that he would have more work for us the following day...as long as we needed the work, he needed the help.

At the end of our work day, we took our belongings and settled into Mr. DeSayeo's barn...it was certainly much larger and much nicer than our former palace. He showed us where there were blankets and oil for the lantern if we chose to use it. He also brought us a snack and a canteen full of cold water.

Blue had lost some of that wild-eyed stare and that nervous-animal jumpiness...maybe it was the apple pie or maybe it was the hard work or more than likely, it was because we would have a bit of respite from walking endlessly in the forest, drinking with the coyotes, sleeping on the ground, dodging rattlers and jumping at every sound. We decided that we would stay for as long as Mr. DeSayeo gave us work or as long as it was safe or until we both knew that it was time to move on.

Mr. DeSayeo spent several evenings with us after we finished our chores, just sitting around, eating bruised apples and talking about nothing all that special. I was happy for the conversation and began to look forward to that time of the day...it was much better than having disturbing conversations with myself, silently reliving several moments of misery and fear. I was anxious to ask him about the bizarre recurring dream I had had, about the birds that weren't really birds at all.

Mr. DeSayeo put his feet up on a tall stack of hay and began to explain that dreams are the left-over thoughts and unfinished business of our waking hours. He told me that sometimes dreaming of birds represented our hopes or things that we want to some-day accomplish. He said that he often had dreams about snakes but that he believed they represented a change in his life, such as the arrival of Blue and me...something that appeared to be terrifying did not necessarily mean danger or any kind of peril, just a change, perhaps a new experience that was meant to strengthen our faith or give one the courage to face something believed to be unpleasant.

Relief flooded my heart...I so wanted to hang on to this piece of wisdom so that I could pull it out and shake hands with it or lean on it the very next time I had a nightmare. I had begun to think of this little trek as a nightmare of its own but maybe now I would be able to look at things from the top down instead of the from the bottom up. Little did I know, I wouldn't have long to wait for the next nightmare.

Blue was still not inclined to talk about himself and I was done with the prodding...I mostly accepted that he had a wounded spirit that would take some time to heal. On the other hand, Mr. DeSayeo was happy to have someone with whom to share stories since he was no longer afraid that we were there to rob him of his store...he was con-

vinced that we were not general store pi-
rates and it made me feel more comfortable
when he was around. I could see that he
was a kind and generous man but I thought
at the time that he was just a little lonely.
A sadness would shadow his face when he
spoke of his uncle as if he were longing for
the family he could barely remember, but it
would pass quickly, then he would nod and
smile,   bid us good night and stroll off to
his own little corner of paradise.

I curled up on my little straw bunk, hoping that I could sleep peacefully after a long
day but again nightmares invaded my restless sleep. Not the recurring dream of the
bird-things...this time, I was trying to cross
a swampy area but there were too many
snakes, writhing and hissing and warning
me to stay away. No two were the same
but there seemed to be no end to them.
No matter which trail I tried to take, they

blocked my path...there were too many of them for me to pass...out of a hollow stump, not more than ten feet away, one of them, much larger than any of the others, poked his head out...he was as black as coal, with eyes like firepits and something akin to feathers around his head...he swayed back and forth as he spoke to the others in a thick oily voice and told them to move aside and let me through.

I tried to hurry away but my feet felt like lead...there were dead bodies of animals and people all around, hundreds of them. From somewhere overhead, I heard a large flock of birds, wings flapping like the great wind just before a storm...suddenly they were screaming, screeching and swooping just above my head as a spasm of fear made itself at home around my heart. I cowered as low to the ground as I could get without lying down but tried to keep my eyes open. When the birds had finally passed, I stood and looked around but saw no bodies and no snakes...the birds had taken all of them away and the trail was clear.

Although the water was knee-deep, I trudged through the swamp...the water was like sludge, thick, black and smelling of long since dead fish innards. I kept getting stuck, frantically pulling myself along, the mud nearly sucking me out of my boots, but at last I made it to the edge and was finally on almost dry land. I sat down on a rock on the edge of the swamp and tried to catch my breath but something kept shaking me and tugging on my sleeve...I swung at it but had unknowingly walloped Blue instead....I snapped fully awake....Blue was holding his jaw and moaning in obvious pain.

I was wide awake now...Blue said I was screeching and beating the air, swinging wildly at something that wasn't there...he had been trying to wake me because it was frightening him...it must have been around 3 or 4 in the morning because it was dark out and there was not a sound, except the slight ruffling of the wind in the trees...the village was still asleep...a storm was com-ing – I could smell the rain in the air. Usually it almost made me giddy, that clean fresh smell of rain, but this time I felt differently, almost sad, as if the thought of rain dampened my spirit.

It had already begun to rain, lightly at first, just a tap, tap, drop, pat and then the soft pattering became harder and harder in a matter of moments. I wanted to stand outside in the downpour and get drenched, to wash away the anxiety, the feeling of loneliness, dregs of bad dreams and too many miles of nothing but bad memories and sore feet, but the rain was cold and the cold was penetrating and I was too afraid of getting sick...I hustled back inside and curled up in my warm blanket.

When I awoke the next time, the rain was still falling, not a downpour but a steady drizzle. I had lost track of the days but I knew that we should go to the store to see what Mr. DeSayeo had for us to do. One of his customers had given me two bits to help him load his wagon...two bits would pay for a meal and I was grateful...2 bits more and I would feel rich.

☾

I was unable to decide if Blue was adjusting to the situation at hand or if he was sinking deeper into his despair...he was silent most of the time and sleeping whenever we had a break from our chores... so far, Mr. DeSayeo has given us work, food, shelter and even a bit of fatherly companionship, none of which we could have gotten on our own... to me that was something to be grateful for...Blue just seemed sad and didn't seem to care about anything. I kept thinking that perhaps we had used up enough of Mr. De-Sayeo's hospitality and that it was time to move on. I attempted to discuss this with Blue but he only shrugged and stared off into vast nothingness...soon he was snoring softly.

I tried to shove aside my frustration, my inability to reach Blue but I could feel my temper straining at the seams...it had up to that point remained mostly dormant, content to allow Blue to work through things on his own, not wanting to humiliate him with constant questions, but I was unsure how much longer I could bear the silent treatment...maybe I was using the wrong approach...the problem was I had no clue what the right approach should be...should I have reminded him that we were in it together? That his troubles were mine? Or should I have waited until it was time to leave and see if he followed? My nerves were a jumbled mess and I noticed that my hands were trembling...I had begun to feel defeated...when the rain cleared, I went to seek guidance from Mr. DeSayeo.

Chapter 4

A strange and heavy sense of loneliness hung over me like a damp wool blanket. I wanted to take Mr. DeSayeo into my confidence and tell him all about my troubles but I just could not bring myself to do it...on the other hand, I could not bring myself to accept going alone, without Blue, and I could not understand how to communicate with him as long as he insisted on being sullen and silent. Although the events which led to my being on this little hike were still vivid in my mind, I tried to soldier on, no matter how weary or how hopeless my efforts...I simply could not curl up in a ball and give up like Blue.

I hurried through the wet street to Mr. DeSayeo's store. I found him chatting with a farmer about crops and how much good the rain would bring...he nodded my way as his bushy eyebrows bounced up and down but he continued his conversation with the farmer...I made myself scarce and found something to do in the back room until he was available.

A few moments later, Mr. DeSayeo came into the back room and I started right away to explain while I still had the strength or before my tongue melted. I wanted him to know just how grateful I was for the work and for giving Blue and me a place to sleep. He waved a hand as if shooing off a gnat but I continued. I told him that I was thinking it was time for us to move on but wanted to hear Blue's thoughts on the matter...I told him I was hoping that he could maybe help me find a way over or around the wall that Blue had built.

Mr. DeSayeo sat down heavily as if burdened with great sadness. As I waited in anguished silence, I realized that I had been clinching and unclenching my teeth, alternating between holding my breath and feeling too much warm air building underneath my heart. Mr. DeSayeo must have sensed my discomfort and told me to try to relax, that my friend would be alright, that there was no way to force Blue to talk until he was ready...he was no doubt afraid of being away from home for the first time and even more afraid to talk about it...all that he and I could do was to show him our understanding, offer him a shoulder and the patience to work things out on his own...there was no way of knowing how long that would take.

Listening to Mr. DeSayeo, everything seemed so simple...I wondered why I had been groping around in the dark for a solution to a problem that wasn't much of a problem...I wanted to laugh out loud as understanding finally landed on my head with a thud.

We walked outside into a bright sunny day. Mr. DeSayeo wanted to know if I was thinking about leaving soon...I mumbled something indecipherable, not yes or no. He told me that when I was ready, that he would show me a way around some of the more tortuous trails, where the ground was so thick with vines and tangled undergrowth, it would make walking almost impossible, but there was a path which led to some railroad tracks...if I followed that path, it would take me to the river where there used to be an old abandoned canoe...if I walked along the tracks, it would be the safest way across but if he canoe was still there and did not leak, it might get us across...just make sure to listen for the sound of the train and not get caught on the tracks or we would have to jump, and it was a long way down. I was so caught up in Mr. DeSayeo's story that I had not noticed that we were headed toward the place where we had eaten the day before...I snapped out of my reverie in time to hear him say 'how about we get some steak, potatoes and ap- ple pie'...I heard a yippee but was shocked to learn that it had come from me.

When I made it back to the barn, Blue was still sleeping. I tried to wake him to ask if he was hungry...I had brought him a ham sand- wich and a slice of apple pie. He opened his eyes but did not seem to recognize me. Finally he stood and went over to one of the canteens and poured water over his head and face...this seemed to bring him back to life so I handed him the sack containing the sandwich and apple pie. A reluctant smile almost made it through but then it disappeared...the sandwich Blue devoured with much enthusiasm. I think I heard a thank you but mostly it was inarticulate muttering as the apple pie also disappeared.

I sat down and waited to see if his fog of depression had lifted. I refused to ask him about his plans for fear that it would plunge him into an even deeper state of despair...it seemed that no matter what the question, it was going to be a thorny subject and it would lead to more silence or even worse, the rush of more internal turmoil...I decided to leave this discussion for another time.

I awoke the next morning feeling as if I had been dragged by a herd of wild horses... the sun seemed to take its time crawling over the horizon as if it was dreading what would come next...I had this roiling feeling in the pit of my belly that today would not be an ordinary day. The recurring night-mare of the bird-like creatures had re-turned with a vengeance so I had tossed and turned most of the night, trying to stay a step ahead of the screeching and snarling, but they were always chasing me and only a few inches away from tearing chunks out of a much-needed body part. I had no watch or calendar so I did not know the day but I knew or felt that it was time to get on with whatever lay ahead...this place no longer felt comfortable and I had the ominous feeling that I was no longer safe here.

I stood and went to find a full canteen so that I could douse myself with enough cold water to wash away the fear and the last fragments of the nightmare...I looked around for Blue but he was already gone...then I pulled on a

pair of semi-clean pants and went outside...
Blue was nowhere in sight.

When I was much younger, my dad told me a story about a bored bird dog, that no matter how much someone shouted at him to go and retrieve the birds, the dog would just stare or yawn and otherwise do nothing. The sight or sound of the birds no longer stirred his once intense enthusiasm to do what he had once lived for...his large, friendly brown eyes were no longer friendly...in fact they were mostly closed, while he napped in a corner or underneath a tree in the cool of the evening. I think the point of the story was that animal or person, no one can convince you or even force you to do what you do not want to do, certainly not until you are ready. The thought of this story made me sad as I was reminded that I was a long way from the person who had told me the story. My heart ached for my family.

I dried my face with the sleeve of my shirt and listened as my stomach grumbled and complained from the lack of breakfast. I hurried out into the sunlight of the new morning, but there was a slight bite to the air, not enough for a chill but enough to let me know that Summer was on its way out and a new Fall would be arriving soon...I needed to go in search of Blue...without having even a clue of where to look, I decided to start with Mr. DeSayeo but when I reached the store, it was closed.

I didn't know exactly where to look for Blue so I just wandered down the street, looking in store windows, past the church and the boarding house, trying to both amuse and distract myself from the disturbing thoughts that were burrowing into my mind. I had never been to the end of town so I started walking and suddenly found myself in the middle of nowhere, a field with scrawny grass and birds streaked with yellow and gray feathers that flew up as I passed by. I looked around but there was nothing to see, especially not Blue...I had left the town behind. I turned around and started back. As I entered the main street, I saw Mr. De-Sayeo heading toward his store...I quicken my pace and arrived at his store almost at the same time as him. His twin caterpillars bounced up and down as he looked a lit-tle startled to see me...then he smiled and waved me inside.

As soon as I was inside, I began chatter-ing like an excited squirrel, that Blue was gone and I had no clue where to look for him. I had walked to the edge of town and looked around but saw no sign of him and no idea of where to go next. Mr. DeSayeo told me to calm down, that he didn't think my friend would just wander off, that it was more than likely he had gotten disoriented and just stayed where he was and hoped that someone would find him and show him the way back.

Outside, the wind seemed to suddenly pick up...I could hear it tossing the tree tops back and forth. I was hungry but my stomach was too queasy to have much of an appe-tite so I waited for Mr. DeSayeo to say that he would either go with me to look for Blue or give me detailed instructions of which way to go. Of course, he could not just shut down his store and go traipsing off into the wild nowhere to look for one lost boy so he handed me an apple and began to explain which trail to take.

At first, the trail was fairly clear as it led away from town and then it became tangled with vines and the road seem to rise and fall which made me unsteady on my feet. I looked up at the sky but the clouds overhead just scudded by with no trace of the sun...I had no idea of which direction I was heading. According to Mr. DeSayeo's instructions, I would find a creek bed soon and hopefully Blue would have found a convenient rock large enough to provide a resting spot for a moment so that he could just sit until someone could find him.

I plodded along, trying not to become entangled in this thick swamp grass - it was what I chose to call it. I turned to look back and could no longer see the town...despite the slight chill in the air, I had begun to sweat. In my haste to leave, I had not remembered to take along a canteen...I had not invited panic along either but he was persistent, whispering in my ears, causing me to stifle a scream...I shook my head trying to clear out the unwanted voice, but all I managed to do was give myself a throbbing headache which caused me to stagger a bit. I put out my hand to stop myself from falling and bumped into a tree...there on the ground, looking distraught and terrified, was Blue. He opened his mouth and made a kind of keening sound which sent shivers down my spine...it was not really a human sound, more like a small wounded animal in agony, but it had come from Blue.

I knelt down beside him to get a closer look... he had dirt on his face and was hugging his knee and rocking back and forth...I tried to assess the problem but this only made the keening louder which ripped through the quiet...he raised the other arm and tried to point at something, but all I could see was more swamp grass and a few scrubby bushes. I told him that we needed to try to get back to town and see if we could find some kind of medical help for him...he began to cry, softly at first, and then great cascades of tears fell down his cheeks.

I struggled to get Blue on his feet, one foot at least...something was wrong with the other one...he could barely put any weight on it. I whispered to him that it would be alright as he clung to me like a jealous lover.

It took what seemed like hours, all but dragging Blue through the tall weeds and grass, small boulders strewn here and there, making walking difficult and most likely painful for Blue, but finally we made it back to Mr. DeSayeo's barn...I gave Blue my apple and then left him sitting on one of the makeshift bunks while I ran to get help.

Thankfully, it didn't take long. Mr. DeSayeo, accompanied by the medicine man, who was tall and well-dressed and with a beard that was almost full. He said that he was a man who was mostly used to working on horses but had done his share of fixing broken legs, snake bites and even a few bullet wounds...he sat down, scratched his chin, opened his bag and got to work on Blue... after a few moments, he announced that Blue had a badly sprained ankle and should not try to walk too much for the next several days. He put some wax on Blue's ankle that smelled like old fish bait, wrapped it in a clean white cloth, then tied it up to that it would not fall off. He told us that was the best he could do and that he would look in on him in a few days...I breathed a sigh of relief when he left and did not ask for pay... we had none to give to him...Mr. DeSayeo said that he would take care of it...I knew this meant that I would have more work to do...it also meant that we would not be leaving for several days, until Blue was able to travel.

In the days that followed, I went to work in Mr. DeSayeo's store and heard many more of his stories. He would pull up a crate, stroke his chin and talk until he heard someone come into the store. He would talk and I would work, moving and re-stacking sacks. Some days he would let me work in the store with him, helping his customers load their groceries onto wagons or buggies. The mornings would fly by quickly, then he and I would mosey off down the street to have lunch...I never tired of the apple pie. We would always take something back for Blue...even though the medicine man said his ankle was much better, he would not leave the barn to go any farther than just outside...he seemed more depressed than ever.

Blue would lay around the barn all day, sleeping on and off, for what seemed like weeks... it was really only a few days. He would eat whatever was given to him and drink the water from the canteens but he refused to leave the barn, not to walk around outside and certainly not to go back to help Mr. DeSayeo in the store. The ankle was better and he was in considerably less pain but it did nothing to lift his spirits.

On that particular morning, as I was about to leave to go to work in Mr. DeSayeo's store,

I told Blue that we were going to leave as soon as he felt up to traveling. I told him that we would need to make as much money as we could because we had no way of knowing what lay on the trail ahead of us or how long it would take for us to reach the next settlement...at some point we would need to get food and possibly a few supplies. Blue looked at me and then suddenly shot to his feet, followed by a loud groan as I watched pain flash across his face...maybe that ankle had not completely healed after all.

Blue sat down again, and looked around as he rubbed his ankle...he shook his head but said nothing...I waited for the tears to flow but this time he only twisted his face into a grimace...I told him that I would find the medicine man and then started to leave.

I told Mr. DeSayeo that Blue seemed to be in great pain and that he would need to see the medicine man again...I kept working while he ran out to see if he could find him... when he came back, he told me that the medicine man was out of town and would be back later in the day. My stomach did a flip and I staggered slightly.

I didn't go back to the barn until late evening. When I walked in, Blue was in the throes of some kind of conniption. He was moaning and flailing his arms, scuttling around on the floor, trying to escape from something only he could see. He began making some type of guttural noise, not exactly a scream but a low-key bellowing. He lay on the floor and his whole body began to shake...a few seconds later, he stopped moving. I just stood there, starring down at him in frozen horror.

I didn't know what to do for him so I threw open the door of the barn and ran as fast as I could. Luckily, a customer was just leaving the store so I ran to tell Mr. DeSayeo that something was terribly wrong with Blue and could he please get the medicine man and come and help.

We were all there – the medicine man, Mr. DeSayeo's customer, Mr. DeSayeo and me, leaning over or kneeling next to Blue. I sat on the floor beside him and his body felt as if it was on fire...the medicine man went to get water and a cloth to wipe his face but Blue was hugging himself and shaking all over so he hardly noticed. He went over to Blue's bunk and picked up a blanket but when he shook it out, something fell to the floor... he knelt down to have a closer look and suddenly his face lit up as if sunlight had just come through the window.

The medicine began working on Blue with a new resolve. He pointed to the floor and told us that he had discovered the cause of Blue's trouble. I rushed over to see what he had found and saw the carcass of a spider on the floor. It had long yellow or sort of brown legs and was about three inches long. The medicine man said that it was a common house spider with a nasty bite but that it was not dangerous...Blue would have a fever and a sore ankle for a few days and then he would be alright.

Blue appeared to be delirious...I wrapped him in the blanket and wiped his face with the cloth and cold water. After a short while, the shakes eased somewhat and he finally opened his eyes but did not seem to recognize me. His eyes darted around the room from one of us to the other and then finally stopped at me again...he didn't seem to know where he was at first but then sat up slowly and asked what had happened. I told him that he had been bitten by a spider but that he would be alright...the medicine man had gone to get some more smelly goo for his ankle and that he would return shortly to take care of him.

The medicine man spread something on Blue's ankle that looked like old apple sauce and smelled like stinky feet, then asked Blue how he felt...he shook his head but his face remained twisted in a grimace...his eyes were red and he had a kind of sickly pallor...when he spoke again, he sounded far away. He said that he had had a dream or a nightmare that a strange creature came at him through a crack in the wall. He said that he had actually struck him but he only ran away for a few minutes and then came at him again. He had some kind of weapon in his hand, something that looked like a short knife which he used to slash at him. He had fought the strange creature with the long hairy fingers until he was too exhausted to fight him any longer... he didn't know he had passed out.

Blue stopped speaking and wrapped his arms around himself as if he was having a chill...I tightened the blanket around him so that he would stop shivering, then we helped him back to his bunk where he lay back down.

Blue was having the nightmare but I too was green around the gills and wearing a dazed look.

We were several days removed from the episode with Blue and the creature with the long brown hairy fingers. He awoke bright and early and he seemed much better after some soup and a good night's rest the night before so when we went back to the store to work, he seemed almost normal or as normal as Blue ever got...the swelling was nearly gone and his ankle didn't seem to bother him...he did not complain of pain at all.

The weather was full on Fall now so I knew that if we did not resume our journey, that we would likely be there until Spring. Mr. DeSayeo said he had grown accustomed to having us around so he didn't encourage us to leave. I was having a strange kind of restlessness, with no parts of an explanation; even though I had enjoyed being around Mr. DeSayeo, I just felt like this was not the place to stay, that there was another place where I would find that much needed something...the name and the real meaning of it escaped me. I didn't think of it as finding a new home but maybe just finding a new place for a new beginning...I could never go back to my home but I couldn't give up hope of seeing my family again.

☾

I worked in Mr. DeSayeo's store but also ran other errands around town... some people gave me food and others gave me 2 bits here and there...I had more money than I had ever had before, close to $6.00 in coin and that made me feel like a grownup.

Later that evening, just as the shadows had begun to crawl across the street, we were locking up for the day...Mr. DeSayeo told Blue and me so sit for a moment and that he has some words of wisdom to share... that was his way of saying that he wanted to say goodbye in his own way without getting weepy or expressing too much emotion. He said that he would give us whatever we needed for the trail and show us the best way to get to the railroad tracks that would take us over the river. As he spoke, he began passing out things...he handed Blue and me each a shirt, heavy enough to be a light jacket, and a blanket each...then he handed us each a small sack of food which included a couple of apples...this he had done since we started working for him...they were usually the ones that were a bit bruised and he didn't want to ask his customers to pay for them. Then suddenly he grew silent. He stared at the floor and began pushing around imaginary bits and pieces of nothing with the toe of his boot...I could see that he was struggling with the words. After a long moment, he announced that he was closing for the night and that we should get a good night's sleep so that we could get an early start the following morning. Unexpectedly, or perhaps not so unexpectedly, he gave us each a hug, then locked the door. Blue and me stood silently staring at him and at each other, trying to find a way to say goodbye...then he gave me one last pat on the shoulder and said goodnight. As I watched him walk away, I felt my heart twist in my chest so hard that I had a moment of dizziness as if the ground beneath my feet had started swaying. When I looked back again, he was gone.

Chapter 5

Blue and me put everything we had together for the trail so that we were ready to leave bright and early the next morning. We had packed our other gifts but we were wearing the jackets he had given us...Mr. DeSayeo has shown us how to make a kind of sled to carry our things so we would not have to over-burden ourselves trying to carry it all... we had somehow accumulated much more stuff than when we started.

The temperature was dropping and the air had a definite bite to it so the jackets felt warm and welcomed. We left Mr. DeSayeo's barn the way we had found it, closed the door for the last time and set off in the direction that he had instructed us to go...or so I thought.

We had sandwiches, hard candy, apples and canteens of cold fresh water so we did not have to worry about finding food or water for a while and could focus all of our energy on finding the railroad tracks that would take us farther west. Before long, we had left the town behind...every now and then, I would look back and see the town fading in the distance and could just barely see the top of something glistening in the sun...maybe Mr. DeSayeo's barn...my pulse quickened at the thought of it...I struggled to keep the sadness at bay.

Blue asked how far away I thought the railroad was and the sound of him speaking caught me by surprise...he seemed a bit more upbeat and I felt hopeful, at least for the moment. I told him that there was no way of knowing how far we had traveled but I had hoped we would find it soon. The sun was not quite overhead so I guess it was around ten o'clock...at noon, the sun would be directly overhead and we would stop to catch our breath and have a snack, providing that we could find a nice wide spot, not too secluded and a nice large boulder to use as a seat or perhaps a convenient fallen tree.

As a kid growing up, I was never especially curious about things around me. I went hunting with my dad once but it was not to test my manly skills on how to survive with just my wits and a hunting knife – it was just to spend time with my dad. I would look after the horses and the other animals around our place but the wildlife never seemed to capture my imagination. However, since the frightening episode with Blue and the spider, I learned to be more aware of my surroundings...I paid attention to the bugs and especially the spiders...I learned that it could make the difference between living and perishing or just avoiding a lot of pain and agony...being out on the trail with no one to help me except another not quite grownup person who knew even less about these things than I did, proved to be a special but a really wild adventure.

We saw deer and coyotes going about their business...I saw flocks of birds flying overhead, I suppose on their way to warmer places...I could hear other forest animals, none of which I could see and was mostly hoping that they could not see me. I jumped at the sound of bees buzzing and the grass rustling. There was always fear from both the known and the unknown, and panic seemed to be a constant companion. Nevertheless, we were out in the wide-open spaces again, a Fall wind blowing the leaves around and two kids who had never spent time alone in the outdoors, were in total awe of all of that wilderness.

After leaving the town behind, after spending so many days in the comfort of Mr. De-Sayeo's barn, being back on the trail was a bit depressing. I thought about going back and having more stew and apple pie but I knew that those days would be memories very soon, great memories, not like the nightmarish memories of weasel face, and I knew that I would have to again adapt to surviving the best way possible, just as

I did when I left my home so many days ago.

We walked at a steady pace and I could tell by the sun that we had been waking for more than 3 hours...I was beginning to feel a bit too warm in my jacket. I was already thinking about the sandwiches in my pack as my belly gave a little growl. Before too long, I would also have to start thinking about where to find shelter before nightfall.

The land was mostly flat but there were a few little hills and we crossed a stream now and then. Just from the distance we had traveled, I knew that the railroad tracks should have been close but so far, no sign of tracks or the slightest rumble of a train.

The sound of rapidly-flowing water reached my ears and I stopped walking and stood still in order to get my bearings. It seemed to be just ahead and to the left of us...we were near a river and would likely stop there for our mid-day snack. On the alert now, I pulled the stick from our little make-shift sled to use not only as a weapon if needed but also to judge how deep the water would be if that was a place where we could cross. The stick was about 6 feet long and Mr. DeSayeo had wrapped and tied a piece of leather from an old saddle around one end so that I could get a better grip on it.

As we approached the sound of rushing water, I saw something shining dully in the sun...the shape of it looked sort of familiar but my brain couldn't quite process it. Blue was right in my tracks as I moved closer, stick held high and ready to swing it at whatever came at me. At about 30 feet away, I could see that it was an overturned canoe...no doubt the one Mr. DeSayeo had mentioned...someone had maybe abandoned it but I wanted to make sure no one was around before I moved it. I inched a little closer.

First I tapped on the top of it...then I pushed it with the stick...when nothing happened, I pointed to a stick on the ground so that

Blue could help me turn it over. Slowly we dragged and tugged until we turned it over...nothing was underneath...just scraggly grass, brown from the lack of sun and rain. I lifted it and stood it up to try to see if it had holes in it...I saw none...it appeared to be about 9 feet in length and had one oar still barely attached to one side. This I decided was an interesting find although I had yet to decide just how interesting – shelter, travel or a bit of both. We dragged the canoe away from the edge of the water just in case a water moccasin got too curious and decided to pay us a visit.

The sun was high, the rays beamed down and felt incredible...I guessed that it was close enough to noon that it would be as good a time as ever to have a sandwich and splash some water over our gums before wading deeper into the underbrush or the swamp so we turned the canoe back over and sat down for lunch.

We were having our sandwiches in silence when I heard a train whistle, low and mournful...it was far away but there was no way of telling just how far. I felt the nerves tighten up in the pit of my stomach...somehow I had veered off the trail or I had taken the wrong trail out of town...I had missed the train tracks altogether...according to the instructions from Mr. DeSayeo, we should have reached the train tracks near the river...once we crossed the river, we would be in another state...I had only a hazy notion that we were heading west but maybe more northwest...after hearing the train whistle, I was no longer sure...I had totally lost my bearings.

The weather was still being kind and co-operative, slightly warm with just a hint of something not quite damp blowing against my face. It was so quiet and still that the sound of flowing water was the loudest sound around us...peaceful but a bit unsettling.

We finished our lunch and I decided that it was time to make some use of the canoe... first I would test the depth of the water... the river wasn't too wide but the water was dark and swirling and I did not want to end up going downstream...Blue was staring at me with a flat gaze or maybe an expectant expression, waiting to see if I would get the problem solved so that we could be on our way.

We wrapped and tied all of our belongings inside the tarp when we were finished with our snack and put everything on our make-shift sled...now all I had to do was figure out what to do with the canoe...I walked up to the edge of the river and put the stick in close to the bank...only about a foot deep...I reached out a bit farther and the water level was more than three feet, more than half the length of my stick...I guessed that by the time I reached the middle of the river, it would be well over my head. It appeared to be about a hundred yards across, I knew we could not risk trying to swim across...the canoe appeared to be the only option.

I handed Blue the oar but as soon as he tried to use it, it broke almost in half...we had to then find another stick that could be used as an oar and I would use my guiding stick. After a bit, we found what we thought to be sufficient and started out again.

We made it all the way across...it was slow going because we had to fight the flow of the river...we encountered a moccasin or two but they went on by so we avoided a fatal encounter. We climbed out of the canoe, testing our footing every step, trying to make sure neither one of us fell or twisted an ankle.

At first we tried carrying the canoe, then we tried pulling it...I just did not want to give it up thinking that we would need it again but hanging on to it proved to be work and made the going much slower...along the way, we decided to just leave it for someone else who might want to use it to get to the other side of the river.

The day dragged on, the sun moved across the brilliantly blue sky and we trudged on through a swampy area. The ground was soggy and made a slushy sound as we walked...Blue told me that alligators lived in the river and like to sleep in areas where they could not be seen...he said that they would attack and swallow us whole...I wasn't sure how he knew that or if he was just making an attempt at being amusing...nevertheless, I was on alert for anything that moved and kept my stick at the ready, but I knew I wanted to get out of the swampy area before nightfall.

As I crept along with grim-faced determination, I could hardly remember the day I left my family...it seemed that I had been wandering for years even though it had only been a few weeks...I was tired in bone and in spirit and still I had only the night to look forward to and more sleeping on the ground. Although I knew the memory of the horrible incident that started me on this trail to nowhere, the feeling of being hunted and the terror of punishment had faded...I had all but accepted that I would not see my home or my family again which sent peals of pain and sadness racing through my heart.

Suddenly Blue was at my elbow, asking me if I was alright...I stifled a shriek and stared at him in amazement...I felt weak in the knees and held on to Blue for support...I could not understand what had caused that strange episode until I remembered that I had been lost in my dark and desolate thoughts...I told Blue that I was alright and finally let go of his arm.

I looked up and discovered that we were approaching a village, a few ramshackle huts strung together, gloomy and ghostly as evening shadows all but surrounded the place. I saw a woman wearing something resembling a shroud, standing beside a man who started toward us, limping slightly. He spoke a few words which I took to mean 'hello' so I nodded and said hello the only way I knew how. He smiled at that and showed several teeth missing but otherwise seemed friendly. The woman waved us forward and tried to usher us inside but Blue was reluctant to move. I nodded toward our

sled and asked if I should leave it outside...
the man nodded back so I left it and went
with him inside.

The woman began to light candles and
lanterns...the place had a long dark hallway and I could see that the entire place
was much in need of some paint and other
kinds of repairs...the house, if one could describe the place as a house, had a window
on each side of the room where the curtains were just barely clinging to the rods
and doors that all seemed to be closed...
it smelled like the swamp that we had just
traveled through, like rotting wood, damp
and musty. There were small square chairs
that looked as if they had been carved from
tree trunks which the man offered to us as
seats...I sat – Blue leaned on me. The woman
brought back something in a jar that could
have been tea...not wanting to appear im-
polite, I accepted it – Blue just shook his
head and said nothing.

For a long moment, there was an uncom-
fortable silence...these people did not seem
to speak English or perhaps they were re-

luctant to talk because they were suspicious of two strange boys. I decided to try to explain that were just wandering through and did not mean to disturb them but perhaps they could point us in the direction of where we could find a place to sleep for the night. With this, the man beamed that smile with the missing teeth and pointed down the long dark hallway...I took that to mean that he was offering us his hospitality and I struggled to find words...should I have said 'no thanks'...we would rather walk on through the night than risk being devoured by whatever is growing on your walls? Instead, I only asked if we could camp out in his yard for the night...there were nods all around and out we went before he had a chance to change his mind.

Blue and I found a less than desirable spot where someone else had built a fire not too many days before...we made a small fire and wrapped up in our blankets. It seemed that I had only been asleep for an hour or so when I was awakened by shouts and screams...it must have been early morning because the sun was just trying to make its way through the straggly trees. I stood up and tried to determine what was happening. I saw the old couple running toward another hut but I chose not to follow...I was not blessed or cursed with morbid curiosity...instead I nudged Blue to make sure he was awake and told him that we should gather our things and be prepared to leave at once.

As we were readying to leave, the old man came over and offered that mostly tooth-less smile...I did not have much to give him but I had about 6 dollars in coins so I gave him one dollar...this he accepted graciously and nodded goodbye.

We hadn't traveled long or very far, maybe two hours of dodging rattlers, alligators, swatting mosquitos the size of prairie hens and negotiating gullies filed with green mossy water, before we saw another village, a town really, [a town that would grow to become a much larger city.] We each gave a small yelp of glee but held the rest of our celebration until we had a chance to see what this town held in store. Maybe we would find another Mr. DeSayeo or perhaps just the opposite, that the town's people would not welcome us and we would have to move on.

On the edge of town was a farmhouse...we stopped there to ask for water before continuing on into the main part of town. A tall man with a large belly was outside rubbing down his horse...he pointed to the well and the dipper and told us to help ourselves.

We each had a drink, thanked the gentleman and turned to leave...he asked us if we were lost or if we were looking for work...we told him that we were looking for a place to find work and settle down. He said that he thought we could probably find both unless we were trouble makers...we assured him that we were not. He tossed a hand in the air goodbye and continued grooming his horse...we continued on toward the town.

Everything about this town struck me as very different from the village where Mr. DeSayeo lived...for one thing, it was much larger. There were signs for things like dry goods, a bank, a livery, restaurants, hotels and a rooming house...we even saw other places of business and stood staring wild-eyed until we drew attention to ourselves. Embarrassed, we continued down the street...Blue said that we should look the place over, as if we really had money in our pockets and were trying to decide on what kind of business to open...we were nothing more than two scruffy kids dragging a make-shift sled that screamed poverty and was barely keeping starvation at bay. As I went past the general store, I looked in the window, just for something to do with my eyes and my heart nearly stopped.

I ducked around a corner and ended up in an alley which ran beside the general store. My mouth had gone dry and the gnawing hunger had been replaced with quaking pangs that ran all the way to my knees...I struggled to catch my breath.

Out of the corner of my eye, I saw her leave the general store...I followed, with Blue nearly tripping over me. I tried to explain but the words just tumbled out and over each other and made no sense. Blue noticed her too and finally realized that it was her that had caused me this confusion and distress and fell in beside me as we followed her. She kept walking until she was all the way down the street about a quarter of a mile... she stopped at a small house on the edge of town. I followed at a short distance but kept my eye on her until she was inside the house. I knew without a doubt that I was going to walk right up to the house and knock on the door...I just didn't know what I was going to say or if the eagle in the pit of my belly would stop flapping his wings long enough for me to be able say anything at all.

Minutes passed. My breathing returned to something approaching normal... now all I had to do was convince my tongue not to fall out when I tried to speak. I stepped up to the door and knocked.

She opened the door and my heart lurched

in my chest. She was beautiful! She was small, with round brown eyes that sort of curved at the corners, and long dark brown hair with golden streaks that hung almost to her waist. A dimple played 'now you see me or maybe not' when she moved her lips...I was so mesmerized I didn't realize she had spoken! She peaked around me and looked at Blue holding that silly looking sled and then back at me... finally I found my voice and said hello.

She was almost identical to my mom except she was younger. When I saw her through the store window, I thought for a second that she was my mom...I couldn't quite un-derstand how or why my mom would have been there in that town...because of course she was not...my imagination and hunger had teamed up to cause me to see some-thing that was not there.

Her name was Kasandia but according to her, people around there insisted on calling her Sandie. I must have been babbling be-cause she finally interrupted me and invited us in.

The house was small but clean and neat. It had yellow curtains and blankets thrown over the chairs and sofa. She was making something in the kitchen that made my mouth water and the rumbling returned to my stomach...I remembered that I had not eaten all day. She must have read my mind or perhaps she saw me drooling and offered me a bowl of whatever smelled like heaven and tasted just as good.

As time went by, Sandie and I spent more and more time together...she was only a year or so older than me but had been on her own for quite some time...she told me that the people in the village had helped her after she had lost her family and although she missed them more than she could possibly describe, she never really felt alone.

Later on, she helped Blue and me find lodging and even jobs. Now that I had money and was a year older, I felt like a real grownup...I knew that that was where I would stay, with Sandie, unless or until we wanted to move to another town.

Many years later, Sandie and I found our own place not too far from where we first met... we are a family now and happy beyond what I ever thought possible. Blue settled down in the town and is now a restaurant owner... he lives in an upstairs loft where he has an art studio and decorates his restaurant with his original artwork...as near as I can tell, he is doing quite well...every now and then, we go over for a visit and talk about our little adventure...we never tired of talking about that amazing apple pie...Blue now serves his own but it's just not the same. His secret re-mained his secret even until today.

"I know who I am

but

I also know

that I am a product

of what I have been

forced to become."

—Green

And Now Enjoy a
Sneak Preview

PANTHER ON THE PROWL

By

Cee McAdams

It was getting close to the weekend and Monday was getting restless. He knew, or thought he knew about a game going on, or in the planning, and he wanted in on it. Word was, that some of the big cats were going to be in this game and the stakes were going to be high...Monday lived under the prevailing theory that he himself was a big cat...more specifically, to him, he was The Top Cat.

To Monday, there was not a pair of dice, a deck of cards or a set of dominoes that he could not master or maneuver to his advantage. He would travel to anyplace, no matter where the game was being held: houses, backrooms, a barn out in the country away from the prying eyes of John Law, wherever he could get in on the action, but only if he knew, or felt that it would be worth his while... this was going to be one of those times.

No one who knew him would dare refer to Monday as a grifter, probably because no one that he knew would be able to tell you what a grifter was, but one with a bit more sophistication or those who were less in-timidated by Monday's impeccable man-ners, his dapper way of dressing, and his cold reptilian stare, would certainly be able to identify him as a charlatan. Monday had a practice of delicately separating those from their money without a bit of blood-letting, but he also had a way of getting in the path of fast-moving vehicles, seemingly without fear of broken bones, mostly his, just to col-lect several thousand dollars from the poor devil who didn't stop in time. He would then parlay those funds into other ventures such as card games or domino games where he would proceed to clean out others who dared not see that ace up his sleeve or that oh so subtle palming of a card at just the right moment, or the wrong one, depending on which side of the pot one was on.

Monday did not hang out in pool rooms although he was just as adept at pool as any of his other 'gaming activities' but this was not his specialty...he did not hang out in alleyways to pick up street games, nor did he hang out on the Riviera...Monday had a reputation to uphold but could not bring himself to admit that he was simply small time...besides that, Monday had 2 young daughters from a previous marriage [the mother had passed away several years prior] and he had not found another woman mentally unstable enough to want to marry him, 2 nice little girls or not. He was, as near as anyone was able to determine, a fairly decent dad. This was due to the fact that other people had their own lives and priorities, and were too busy to pay close attention to Monday...they didn't know that he just had a natural predisposition for using people for his own purposes, which usually meant financial gain...the daughters were just naturally going to figure into his plan.

It was around 10 on this Friday morning, the end of the week of Spring break and the girls were sleeping late. Monday didn't wake them but knew he had to find out soon what their plans were for the day. They were ages 17 & 18. The older one, who had the misfortune of being named Caledonia after some long dead relative, was called Cal which she much preferred to being called by her middle name Marie, and the first name was out of the question entirely... the other one was named Shannan but her father insisted on calling her Shadow...he joked that she would stick so close to him that he could not separate his shadow from hers...fact or fiction, it hardly mattered to Monday or Shannan or to anyone else for that matter.

Early in her life, Cal has suffered a devasting illness and had been forced to miss almost an entire year of school...as a result of this,

Shannan had gained on her and they were both in the same grade now and both were scheduled to graduate at the same time. To Monday, this meant twice as many and twice as much of everything...his girls were important but Monday's gambling activities took precedence over everything else...to him, the solution was to incorporate them into the weekend's activities...he just had to formulate a plan on just how to do it without tipping his hand or jeopardizing their safety, while pursuing his professional fun, a proverbial killing, an outright fleecing of some very fat cats.

Monday sat down at the kitchen table and unwrapped a cigar while he pondered this... he knew there would be at least a 50 grand jackpot...he had been told that the buy-in was 10 grand each so for just 5 players, he was going to be in the money. He had his buy-in...he had put it aside from his last run-in with a taxi cab where he sustained minor injuries and a torn sports jacket...this little get-together had netted him $16,000 after the dust had settled. Not a bad days' pay for tripping over air and falling in front of an 8-cylinder vehicle. This one was much more profitable than the one several months before...he had only gotten $6800 from that one...he only rolled off the bumper of a semi who had the presence of mind to stop short of hitting him, so Monday had hit the truck instead...after all, he had needed the money...of course working anything except his fingers was out of the question...getting a regular job and working for a living was for other people who didn't have his skills with the bones and cards.

A few minutes later, the girls came down the stairs and gave him a gentle hug...this never failed to make his eyes light up and his eyebrows bounce up and down. They went into the kitchen and each came back with a bowl of cereal. He looked at each one in turn before asking what they had in mind for the day and into the evening...

much to his great delight they told him that they wanted to spend the day and possibly into the evening with him since it was the last day of their freedom before school started again...specific activities could be determined later. Seeming to drag the words out as if they were causing him great pain, he assured them that he had just the thing...he had been invited to a small soiree where there would be drinks and snacks and he thought the girls would enjoy it. They practically levitated out of their chairs to smother him with hugs and kisses. There was a slight ringing in his ears as his cigar began to spin...he thought it might ignite on its own.

Monday told the girls that they could go to the mall and find something to wear...nothing too alluring but something 'nice.' He didn't seem to realize that to a teenage girl, this meant something totally different from what he assumed it meant. He gave each of them $200 and told them that they had to be back by 5...he wanted to be at the party by 6 or so. A kiss on the cheek from each of them and off they went. Now he could take a nap and be fully rested for his finest hour.

Monday sashayed in with a daughter on each arm...a thrill passed through him as he felt his pulse kick up a notch or two...of course no one knew these were his daughters and he was not about to inform anyone...these girls could easily have passed for 24 or 25, which is exactly what Monday had in mind.

After a short turn around the room and introducing the girls to a few people, he showed them to the buffet table...it was about time for the game to begin. The girls had their orders and knew exactly when to make an appearance to 'observe' and exactly what to do and when to do it.

They sat across the room from where the game was going on and finished a small snack, nibbling on this little delicacy and that one...for teenage girls, this was not their idea of real food...pizza or tacos would have fit the bill just nicely...still they were excited to be a part of Monday's evening and decided not to complain...after all, they had been promised a lot of money, the senior trip and a chance to buy anything they would like for graduation...they would not blow this opportunity to have nice fat wallets plus make Monday proud.

The game was going smoothly...Monday lost out on the first round, mostly on purpose, what he had once referred to as 'priming the pump.' The next hand was his and then he began to win one hand after the other. The girls had made their appearance and most of the other players were distracted by Monday's ladies and their attention wavered just slightly, enough to miss out on Monday's little tricks...he knew them all: memorization, reverse cuts, bottom drags and a few more he used as the game went along that he had practiced and perfected over the years.

The girls moved around the table, smiling and winking at first one small wizened guy, and then another with a beard, and one who wore a tie-dyed shirt loud enough to cause hearing loss...you could definitely hear it all the way across the room. Finally, a little old guy who looked like a professional chef, with a floppy moustache and a mischievous smile, announced that he was out of coin or out of snuff or out of both and simply had to have a bathroom break...besides, he had had enough for one night. The game was called to a halt and Monday raked in his winnings with a bit of a theatrical flair. He nodded his thanks to the other players for a titillating game, stood and strode out the door, a daughter on each arm.

Monday made it back to his vehicle and sat for a moment waiting for the knot in his stomach to unclench...the girls were anxious to get home... Monday had promised them a share of his winnings for being his 'guests,' neither being aware that they had just been a part of something under-handed and devious...neither was aware that this kind of

activity was a part of Monday's daily life, a malignancy that had made itself at home in his heart. To them, it was just a night out with dad, wearing cute dresses and eating some strange food...the money would just be a nice bonus.

When they made it home and the money was counted, Monday had won back his initial 10 grand plus 54 grand...it had been a good night indeed...he was more than happy to share the wealth so he gave each daughter $2000...this in addition to offering to pay for whatever their needs were for graduation...the rest he would squirrel away for the next time he needed a buy-in for a big game.

"Never

Play

Hopscotch

With a

Kangaroo."

—Cee McAdams